Thy Sweet Love Remembered

Thy Sweet Love Remembered

The Most Beautiful Love Poems

and Sonnets of

William Shakespeare

Selected and Arranged by Dorothy Price

With Drawings by Bill Greer

 HALLMARK EDITIONS

Thy Sweet Love Remembered

SONNET 1

From fairest creatures we desire increase,

That thereby beauty's rose might never die,

But as the riper should by time decrease,

His tender heir might bear his memory;

But thou, contracted to thine own bright eyes,

Feed'st thy light's flame with self-substantial fuel,

Making a famine where abundance lies,

Thyself thy foe, to thy sweet self too cruel.

Thou that art now the world's fresh ornament

And only herald to the gaudy spring,

Within thine own bud buriest thy content,

And, tender churl, mak'st waste in niggarding.

Pity the world, or else this glutton be,

To eat the world's due, by the grave and thee.

SONNET II

When forty winters shall besiege thy brow,

And dig deep trenches in thy beauty's field,

Thy youth's proud livery, so gaz'd on now,

Will be a tatter'd weed of small worth held.

Then being ask'd where all thy beauty lies,

Where all the treasure of thy lusty days,

To say within thine own deep-sunken eyes

Were an all-eating shame and thriftless praise.

How much more praise deserv'd thy beauty's use,

If thou couldst answer 'This fair child of mine

Shall sum my count, and make my old excuse'

Proving his beauty by succession thine!

This were to be new made when thou art old,

And see the blood warm when thou feel'st it cold.

SONNET VIII

Music to hear, why hear'st thou music sadly?

Sweets with sweets war not, joy delights in joy.

Why lov'st thou that which thou receiv'st not gladly,

Or else receiv'st with pleasure thine annoy?

If the true concord of well-tuned sounds,

By union married, do offend thine ear,

They do but sweetly chide thee, who confounds

In singleness the parts that thou shouldst bear.

Mark how one string, sweet husband to another,

Strikes each in each by mutual ordering;

Resembling sire, and child, and happy mother,

Who, all in one, one pleasing note do sing;

Whose speechless song, being many, seeming one,

Sings this to thee: 'Thou single wilt prove none'.

SONNET XIV

Not from the stars do I my judgment pluck,

And yet methinks I have astronomy;

But not to tell of good or evil luck,

Of plagues, of dearths, or seasons' quality;

Nor can I fortune to brief minutes tell,

Pointing to each his thunder, rain, and wind,

Or say with princes if it shall go well

By oft predict that I in heaven find;

But from thine eyes my knowledge I derive,

And, constant stars, in them I read such art

As truth and beauty shall together thrive,

If from thy self to store thou wouldst convert.

Or else of thee this I prognosticate:

Thy end is truth's and beauty's doom and date.

SONNET XV

When I consider every thing that grows

Holds in perfection but a little moment,

That this huge stage presenteth nought but shows

Whereon the stars in secret influence comment;

When I perceive that men as plants increase,

Cheered and check'd even by the self-same sky,

Vaunt in their youthful sap, at height decrease,

And wear their brave state out of memory;

Then the conceit of this inconstant stay

Set you most rich in youth before my sight,

Where wasteful Time debateth with Decay

To change your day of youth to sullied night;

And all in war with Time for love of you,

As he takes from you, I engraft you new.

SONNET XVIII

Shall I compare thee to a summer's day?

Thou art more lovely and more temperate.

Rough winds do shake the darling buds of May,

And summer's lease hath all too short a date:

Sometime too hot the eye of heaven shines,

And often is his gold complexion dimm'd;

And every fair from fair sometime declines,

By chance or nature's changing course untrimm'd;

But thy eternal summer shall not fade,

Nor lose possession of that fair thou owest;

Nor shall Death brag thou wander'st in his shade,

When in eternal lines to time thou grow'st.

So long as men can breathe, or eyes can see,

So long lives this, and this gives life to thee.

SONNET XXII

My glass shall not persuade me I am old,

So long as youth and thou are of one date;

But when in thee time's furrows I behold,

Then look I death my days should expiate.

For all that beauty that doth cover thee

Is but the seemly raiment of my heart,

Which in thy breast doth live, as thine in me:

How can I then be elder than thou art?

O, therefore, love, be of thyself so wary

As I, not for myself, but for thee will;

Bearing thy heart, which I will keep so chary

As tender nurse her babe from faring ill.

Presume not on thy heart when mine is slain;

Thou gavest me thine, not to give back again.

SONNET XXV

Let those who are in favour with their stars

Of public honour and proud titles boast,

Whilst I, whom fortune of such triumph bars,

Unlook'd for joy in that I honour most.

Great princes' favourites their fair leaves spread

But as the marigold at the sun's eye;

And in themselves their pride lies buried,

For at a frown they in their glory die.

The painful warrior famoused for fight,

After a thousand victories once foil'd,

Is from the book of honour razed quite,

And all the rest forgot for which he toil'd.

Then happy I, that love and am beloved

Where I may not remove nor be removed.

SONNET XXIX

When in disgrace with fortune and men's eyes,

I all alone beweep my outcast state,

And trouble deaf heaven with my bootless cries,

And look upon myself, and curse my fate,

Wishing me like to one more rich in hope,

Featured like him, like him with friends possess'd,

Desiring this man's art and that man's scope,

With what I most enjoy contented least;

Yet in these thoughts myself almost despising,

Haply I think on thee, and then my state,

Like to the lark at break of day arising

From sullen earth, sings hymns at heaven's gate;

For thy sweet love remember'd such wealth brings

That then I scorn to change my state with kings.

SONNET XXX

When to the sessions of sweet silent thought

I summon up remembrance of things past,

I sigh the lack of many a thing I sought,

And with old woes new wail my dear time's waste:

Then can I drown an eye, unused to flow,

For precious friends hid in death's dateless night,

And weep afresh love's long since cancell'd woe,

And moan the expense of many a vanish'd sight:

Then can I grieve at grievances foregone,

And heavily from woe to woe tell o'er

The sad account of fore-bemoaned moan,

Which I new pay as if not paid before.

But if the while I think on thee, dear friend,

All losses are restored and sorrows end.

SONNET XXXI

Thy bosom is endeared with all hearts,

Which I by lacking have supposed dead;

And there reigns love, and all love's loving parts,

And all those friends which I thought buried.

How many a holy and obsequious tear

Hath dear religious love stol'n from mine eye,

As interest of the dead, which now appear

But things removed that hidden in thee lie!

Thou art the grave where buried love doth live,

Hung with the trophies of my lovers gone,

Who all their parts of me to thee did give;

That due of many now is thine alone.

Their images I loved I view in thee,

And thou, all they, hast all the all of me.

SONNET XXXV

No more be griev'd at that which thou hast done:

Roses have thorns, and silver fountains mud;

Clouds and eclipses stain both moon and sun,

And loathsome canker lives in sweetest bud.

All men make faults, and even I in this,

Authorizing thy trespass with compare,

Myself corrupting, salving thy amiss,

Excusing thy sins more than thy sins are;

For to thy sensual fault I bring in sense –

The adverse party is thy advocate –

And 'gainst myself a lawful plea commence;

Such civil war is in my love and hate

That I an accessary needs must be

To that sweet thief which sourly robs from me.

SONNET XL

Take all my loves, my love, yea, take them all;

What hast thou then more than thou hadst before?

No love, my love, that thou mayst true love call,

All mine was thine before thou hadst this more.

Then, if for my love thou my love receivest,

I cannot blame thee for my love thou usest;

But yet be blamed, if thou thyself deceivest

By wilful taste of what thyself refusest.

I do forgive thy robbery, gentle thief,

Although thou steal thee all my poverty;

And yet, love knows, it is a greater grief

To bear love's wrong than hate's known injury.

Lascivious grace, in whom all ill well shows,

Kill me with spites; yet we must not be foes.

SONNET XLIV

If the dull substance of my flesh were thought,

Injurious distance should not stop my way;

For then, despite of space, I would be brought

From limits far remote, where thou dost stay.

No matter then, although my foot did stand

Upon the farthest earth remov'd from thee,

For nimble thought can jump both sea and land

As soon as think the place where he would be.

But ah! thought kills me that I am not thought,

To leap large lengths of miles when thou art gone,

But that, so much of earth and water wrought,

I must attend time's leisure with my moan,

Receiving nought by elements so slow

But heavy tears, badges of either's woe.

SONNET XLV

The other two, slight air and purging fire,

Are both with thee, wherever I abide;

The first my thought, the other my desire,

These present-absent with swift motion slide.

For when these quicker elements are gone

In tender embassy of love to thee,

My life, being made of four, with two alone

Sinks down to death, oppress'd with melancholy;

Until life's composition be recured

By those swift messengers return'd from thee,

Who even but now come back again, assured

Of thy fair health, recounting it to me.

This told, I joy; but then no longer glad,

I send them back again, and straight grow sad.

SONNET XLVII

Betwixt mine eye and heart a league is took,

And each doth good turns now unto the other.

When that mine eye is famish'd for a look,

Or heart in love with sighs himself doth smother,

With my love's picture then my eye doth feast

And to the painted banquet bids my heart;

Another time mine eye is my heart's guest

And in his thoughts of love doth share a part:

So, either by thy picture or my love,

Thyself away art present still with me;

For thou not farther than my thoughts canst move,

And I am still with them and they with thee;

Or, if they sleep, thy picture in my sight

Awakes my heart to heart's and eye's delight.

SONNET L

How heavy do I journey on the way,

When what I seek – my weary travel's end –

Doth teach that ease and that repose to say,

'Thus far the miles are measured from thy friend!'

The beast that bears me, tired with my woe,

Plods dully on, to bear that weight in me,

As if by some instinct the wretch did know

His rider loved not speed, being made from thee.

The bloody spur cannot provoke him on

That sometimes anger thrusts into his hide;

Which heavily he answers with a groan,

More sharp to me than spurring to his side;

For that same groan doth put this in my mind:

My grief lies onward, and my joy behind.

SONNET LV

Not marble, nor the gilded monuments

Of princes, shall outlive this powerful rhyme;

But you shall shine more bright in these contents

Than unswept stone, besmear'd with sluttish time.

When wasteful war shall statues overturn,

And broils root out the work of masonry,

Nor Mars his sword nor war's quick fire shall burn

The loving record of your memory.

'Gainst death and all-oblivious enmity

Shall you pace forth; your praise shall still find room

Even in the eyes of all posterity

That wear this world out to the ending doom.

So, till the judgement that yourself arise,

You live in this, and dwell in lovers' eyes.

SONNET LVII

Being your slave, what should I do but tend

Upon the hours and times of your desire?

I have no precious time at all to spend,

Nor services to do, till you require.

Nor dare I chide the world-without-end hour

Whilst I, my sovereign, watch the clock for you,

Nor think the bitterness of absence sour

When you have bid your servant once adieu;

Nor dare I question with my jealous thought

Where you may be, or your affairs suppose,

But, like a sad slave, stay and think of nought

Save where you are how happy you make those.

So true a fool is love that in your will,

Though you do any thing, he thinks no ill.

SONNET LVIII

That god forbid that made me first your slave,

I should in thought control your times of pleasure,

Or at your hand the account of hours to crave,

Being your vassal, bound to stay your leisure!

O, let me suffer, being at your beck,

The imprison'd absence of your liberty;

And patience, tame to sufferance, bide each check,

Without accusing you of injury.

Be where you list, your charter is so strong

That you yourself may privilege your time

To what you will; to you it doth belong

Yourself to pardon of self-doing crime.

I am to wait, though waiting so be hell;

Not blame your pleasure, be it ill or well.

SONNET LX

Like as the waves make towards the pebbled shore,

So do our minutes hasten to their end;

Each changing place with that which goes before,

In sequent toil all forwards do contend.

Nativity, once in the main of light,

Crawls to maturity, wherewith being crown'd,

Crooked eclipses 'gainst his glory fight,

And Time that gave doth now his gift confound.

Time doth transfix the flourish set on youth

And delves the parallels in beauty's brow,

Feeds on the rarities of nature's truth,

And nothing stands but for his scythe to mow.

And yet to times in hope my verse shall stand,

Praising thy worth, despite his cruel hand.

SONNET LXI

Is it thy will thy image should keep open

My heavy eyelids to the weary night?

Dost thou desire my slumbers should be broken,

While shadows like to thee do mock my sight?

Is it thy spirit that thou send'st from thee

So far from home into my deeds to pry,

To find out shames and idle hours in me,

The scope and tenour of thy jealousy?

O, no! thy love, though much, is not so great:

It is my love that keeps mine eye awake;

Mine own true love that doth my rest defeat,

To play the watchman ever for thy sake.

For thee watch I whilst thou dost wake elsewhere,

From me far off, with others all too near.

SONNET LXXIII

That time of year thou mayst in me behold

When yellow leaves, or none, or few, do hang

Upon those boughs which shake against the cold,

Bare ruin'd choirs, where late the sweet birds sang.

In one thou see'st the twilight of such day

As after sunset fadeth in the west;

Which by and by black night doth take away,

Death's second self, that seals up all in rest.

In me thou see'st the glowing of such fire,

That on the ashes of his youth doth lie,

As the death-bed whereon it must expire,

Consumed with that which it was nourish'd by.

This thou perceivest, which makes

                    thy love more strong,

To love that well which thou must leave ere long.

SONNET LXXV

So are you to my thoughts as food to life,

Or sweet-season'd showers are to the ground;

And for the peace of you I hold such strife

As 'twixt a miser and his wealth is found:

Now proud as an enjoyer, and anon

Doubting the filching age will steal his treasure;

Now counting best to be with you alone,

Then better'd that the world may see my pleasure;

Sometime all full with feasting on your sight,

And by and by clean starved for a look;

Possessing or pursuing no delight

Save what is had or must from you be took.

Thus do I pine and surfeit day by day,

Or gluttoning on all, or all away.

SONNET LXXX

O, how I faint when I of you do write,

Knowing a better spirit doth use your name

And in the praise thereof spends all his might

To make me tongue-tied, speaking of your fame!

But since your worth, wide as the ocean is,

The humble as the proudest sail doth bear,

My saucy bark, inferior far to his,

On your broad main doth wilfully appear.

Your shallowest help will hold me up afloat,

Whilst he upon your soundless deep doth ride;

Or, being wreck'd, I am a worthless boat,

He of tall building and of goodly pride.

Then if he thrive, and I be cast away,

The worst was this: my love was my decay.

SONNET LXXXVIII

When thou shalt be disposed to set me light,

And place my merit in the eye of scorn,

Upon thy side against myself I'll fight,

And prove thee virtuous, though thou art forsworn.

With mine own weakness being best acquainted,

Upon thy part I can set down a story

Of faults conceal'd, wherein I am attainted;

That thou in losing me shall win much glory.

And I by this will be a gainer too;

For bending all my living thoughts on thee,

The injuries that to myself I do,

Doing thee vantage, double-vantage me.

Such is my love, to thee I so belong,

That for thy right myself will bear all wrong.

SONNET LXXXIX

Say that thou didst forsake me for some fault,

And I will comment upon that offence;

Speak of my lameness, and I straight will halt;

Against thy reasons making no defence.

Thou canst not, love, disgrace me half so ill,

To set a form upon desired change,

As I'll myself disgrace, knowing thy will.

I will acquaintance strangle and look strange,

Be absent from thy walks, and in my tongue

Thy sweet beloved name no more shall dwell,

Lest I, too much profane, should do it wrong,

And haply of our old acquaintance tell.

For thee, against myself I'll vow debate,

For I must ne'er love him whom thou dost hate.

SONNET XCIII

So shall I live, supposing thou art true,

Like a deceived husband; so love's face

May still seem love to me, though alter'd new –

Thy looks with me, thy heart in other place.

For there can live no hatred in thine eye;

Therefore in that I cannot know thy change.

In many's looks the false heart's history

Is writ in moods and frowns and wrinkles strange;

But heaven in thy creation did decree

That in thy face sweet love should ever dwell;

Whate'er thy thoughts or thy heart's workings be,

Thy looks should nothing thence but sweetness tell.

How like Eve's apple doth thy beauty grow,

If thy sweet virtue answer not thy show!

SONNET CXIII

Since I left you, mine eye is in my mind;

And that which governs me to go about

Doth part his function, and is partly blind,

Seems seeing, but effectually is out;

For it no form delivers to the heart

Of bird, of flow'r, or shape, which it doth latch;

Of his quick objects hath the mind no part,

Nor his own vision holds what it doth catch;

For if it see the rudest or gentlest sight,

The most sweet favour or deformed'st creature,

The mountain or the sea, the day or night,

The crow or dove, it shapes them to your feature:

Incapable of more, replete with you,

My most true mind thus mak'th mine eye untrue.

SONNET CXVI

Let me not to the marriage of true minds

Admit impediments. Love is not love

Which alters when it alteration finds,

Or bends with the remover to remove.

O, no! it is an ever-fixed mark,

That looks on tempests and is never shaken;

It is the star to every wand'ring bark,

Whose worth's unknown although

his height be taken.

Love's not Time's fool, though rosy lips and cheeks

Within his bending sickle's compass come;

Love alters not with his brief hours and weeks,

But bears it out even to the edge of doom.

If this be error, and upon me proved,

I never writ, nor no man ever loved.

SONNET CXX

That you were once unkind befriends me now,

And for that sorrow which I then did feel

Needs must I under my transgression bow,

Unless my nerves were brass or hammer'd steel.

For if you were by my unkindness shaken,

As I by yours, you've pass'd a hell of time;

And I, a tyrant, have no leisure taken

To weigh how once I suffer'd in your crime.

O, that our night of woe might have remember'd

My deepest sense how hard true sorrow hits,

And soon to you, as you to me, then tender'd

The humble salve which wounded bosoms fits!

But that your trespass now becomes a fee;

Mine ransoms yours, and yours must ransom me.

SONNET CXXX

My mistress' eyes are nothing like the sun;

Coral is far more red than her lips' red;

If snow be white, why then her breasts are dun;

If hairs be wires, black wires grow on her head.

I have seen roses damask'd, red and white,

But no such roses see I in her cheeks;

And in some perfumes is there more delight

Than in the breath that from my mistress reeks.

I love to hear her speak, yet well I know

That music hath a far more pleasing sound;

I grant I never saw a goddess go –

My mistress, when she walks, treads on the ground.

And yet, by heaven, I think my love as rare

As any she belied with false compare.

SONNET CXXXVIII

When my love swears that she is made of truth,

I do believe her, though I know she lies,

That she might think me some untutor'd youth,

Unlearned in the world's false subtleties.

Thus vainly thinking that she thinks me young,

Although she knows my days are past the best,

Simply I credit her false-speaking tongue;

On both sides thus is simple truth suppress'd.

But wherefore says she not she is unjust?

And wherefore say not I that I am old?

O, love's best habit is in seeming trust,

And age in love loves not to have years told.

Therefore I lie with her and she with me,

And in our faults by lies we flatter'd be.

SONNET CXLV

Those lips that Love's own hand did make

Breathed forth the sound that said 'I hate'

To me that languish'd for her sake;

But when she saw my woeful state,

Straight in her heart did mercy come,

Chiding that tongue that ever sweet

Was used in giving gentle doom;

And taught it thus anew to greet:

'I hate' she alter'd with an end

That follow'd it as gentle day

Doth follow night, who like a fiend

From heaven to hell is flown away:

'I hate' from hate away she threw,

And saved my life, saying 'not you.'

SONNET CXLIX

Canst thou, O cruel! say I love thee not,

When I against myself with thee partake?

Do I not think on thee when I forgot

Am of myself, all tyrant for thy sake?

Who hateth thee that I do call my friend?

On whom frown'st thou that I do fawn upon?

Nay, if thou lour'st on me, do I not spend

Revenge upon myself with present moan?

What merit do I myself respect

That is so proud thy service to despise,

When all my best doth worship thy defect,

Commanded by the motion of thine eyes?

But, love, hate on, for now I know thy mind:

Those that can see thou lovest, and I am blind.

Poems And Selections From The Plays

From KING HENRY VIII

Song

Orpheus with his lute made trees,

And the mountain tops that freeze,

Bow themselves when he did sing:

To his music plants and flowers

Ever sprung, as sun and showers

There had made a lasting spring.

Every thing that heard him play,

Even the billows of the sea,

Hung their heads, and then lay by.

In sweet music is such art,

Killing care and grief of heart

Fall asleep, or hearing die.

From HAMLET

Ophelia's Song

How should I your true love know

From another one?

By his cockle hat and staff,

And his sandal shoon.

He is dead and gone, lady,

He is dead and gone;

At his head a grass-green turf,

At his heels a stone.

White his shroud as the mountain snow –

Larded with sweet flowers;

Which bewept to the grave did not go

With true-love showers.

From CYMBELINE

Song

Hark, hark! the lark at heaven's gate sings,

And Phoebus 'gins arise,

His steeds to water at those springs

On chaliced flowers that lies;

And winking Mary-buds begin

To ope their golden eyes;

With every thing that pretty is,

My lady sweet arise: Arise, arise!

From TWELFTH NIGHT

O Mistress Mine

O mistress mine, where are you roaming?

O, stay and hear; your true love's coming,

That can sing both high and low:

Trip no further, pretty sweeting;

Journeys end in lovers meeting,

Every wise man's son doth know.

What is love? 'tis not hereafter;

Present mirth hath present laughter;

What's to come is still unsure:

In delay there lies no plenty;

Then come kiss me, sweet and twenty,

Youth's a stuff will not endure.

From LOVE'S LABOR'S LOST

So Sweet A Kiss

So sweet a kiss the golden sun gives not

To those fresh morning drops upon the rose,

As thy eye-beams, when their fresh rays have smote

The night of dew that on my cheeks down flows:

Nor shines the silver moon one half so bright

Through the transparent bosom of the deep,

As doth thy face through tears of mine give light;

Thou shinest in every tear that I do weep:

No drop but as a coach doth carry thee;

So ridest thou triumphing in my woe.

Do but behold the tears that swell in me,

And they thy glory through my grief will show:

But do not love thyself; then thou wilt keep

My tears for glasses, and still make me weep.

O queen of queens! how far dost thou excel,

No thought can think, nor tongue

                            of mortal tell.

From ROMEO AND JULIET

What light through yonder window breaks?

But, Soft! What light through yonder window breaks?

It is the east, and Juliet is the sun.

Arise, fair sun, and kill the envious moon,

Who is already sick and pale with grief

That thou her maid are far more fair than she.

Be not her maid, since she is envious;

Her vestal livery is but sick and green,

And none but fools do wear it; cast it off.

It is my lady; O, it is my love!

O that she knew she were!

She speaks, yet she says nothing. What of that?

Her eye discourses; I will answer it.

I am too bold, 'tis not to me she speaks;

Two of the fairest stars in all the heaven,

Having some business, do entreat her eyes

To twinkle in their spheres till thy return.

What if her eyes were there, they in her head?

The brightness of her cheek would shame

those stars,

As daylight doth a lamp; her eyes in heaven

Would through the airy region stream

so bright

That birds would sing, and think it were

not night.

See how she leans her cheek upon her hand!

That I might touch that cheek!

From THE TWO GENTLEMEN OF VERONA

Song

Who is Silvia? what is she,

That all our swains commend her?

Holy, fair, and wise is she;

The heaven such grace did lend her,

That she might admired be.

Is she kind as she is fair?

For beauty lives with kindness.

Love doth to her eyes repair,

To help him of his blindness,

And, being help'd, inhabits there.

Then to Silvia let us sing,

That Silvia is excelling;

She excels each mortal thing

Upon the dull earth dwelling:

To her let us garlands bring.

From ANTONY AND CLEOPATRA

Cleopatra: I dreamt there was an Emperor Antony –

O, such another sleep, that I might see

But such another man!

Dolabella: If it might please ye –

Cleopatra: His face was as the heav'ns,

                                    and therein stuck

A sun and moon, which kept their course

And lighted the little O, the earth.

Dolabella: Most sovereign creature –

Cleopatra: His legs bestrid the ocean; his rear'd arm

Crested the world. His voice was propertied

As all the tuned spheres, and that to friends;

But when he meant to quail and shake the orb,

He was as rattling thunder. For his bounty,

There was no winter in't; an autumn 'twas

That grew the more by reaping. His delights

Were dolphin-like: they show'd his back above

The element they liv'd in. In his livery

Walk'd crowns and crownets; realms and islands

Were as plates dropp'd from his pocket.

Dolabella: Cleopatra –

Cleopatra: Think you there was or might be

Such a man as this I dreamt of?

Dolabella: Gentle madam, no.

Cleopatra: You lie, up to the hearing of the gods.

But if there be nor ever were one such,

It's past the size of dreaming. Nature wants stuff

To vie strange forms with fancy; yet t' imagine

An Antony were nature's piece 'gainst fancy,

Condemning shadows quite.

Set in Shakespeare roman,

designed by Gudrun Zapf von Hesse

exclusively for Hallmark Editions

and appearing for the first time in this book.